A MUSIC
LOVER'S
DIARY

MUSIC LOVER _____

DIARY KEPT BETWEEN _____ AND _____

A MUSIC LOVER'S DIARY

FIREFLY BOOKS

A Music Lover's Diary
ISBN 1-55209-024-8

🌐
A Firefly Book

Published by Firefly Books Ltd., 3680 Victoria Park Avenue,
Willowdale, Ontario, Canada M2H 3K1

Published in the U.S. by Firefly Books (U.S.) Inc.
P.O. Box 1338, Ellicott Station, Buffalo, New York 14205

Conceived and edited by Shelagh Wallace
Design and original illustrations by Scott McKowen

Acknowledgements
We wish to thank those publishers who have given their permission
to reproduce excerpts from works still in copyright. If anyone has been
unintentionally omitted, we offer our apologies and ask that you notify
the publisher so you may be included in future editions.

Quotations by Henry David Thoreau and Robert Browning reprinted with
permission of Schirmer Books, an imprint of Simon & Schuster Macmillan,
from *Dictionary of Musical Quotations*, compiled by Ian Crofton and Donald
Fraser. Copyright ©1985 by Ian Crofton and Donald Fraser.

Quotations by Friedrich Nietzsche, Pete Seeger, Dizzy Gillespie, Mel Brooks,
Ringo Starr, Cole Porter, Robert Schumann, and Robert Benchley are reprint-
ed from the book *The Music Lover's Quotation Book* compiled by Kathleen
Kimball and published by Sound And Vision (Canada) in 1990.

Quotation by Aaron Copland reprinted with permission of Little, Brown
& Co. (UK), from the book *The Tender Tyrant* by Alan Kendall, copyright
©1976.

Illustration on page 50 from a poster entitled "Beethoven Quartet Cycle"
for a year-long concert tour in 1989-90 by the Juilliard String Quartet,
featuring the composer's complete string quartets.

Printed in Canada

TABLE OF CONTENTS

Music is a moral law. It gives a soul to the universe, wings to the mind, flight to the imagination, a charm to sadness, gaiety and life to everything. It is the essence of order, and leads to all that is good, just and beautiful, of which it is the invisible, but nevertheless, dazzling, passionate, and eternal form. PLATO

A true music lover is one who on hearing a blonde soprano singing in the bathtub puts his ear to the keyhole.

ANONYMOUS

After playing Chopin, I feel as if I had been weeping over sins that I had never committed, and mourning over tragedies that were not my own. Music always seems to me to produce that effect. It creates for one a past of which one has been ignorant and fills one with a sense of sorrows that have been hidden from one's tears. OSCAR WILDE

MUSIC
NOTES

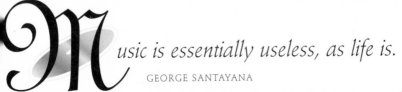

usic is essentially useless, as life is.

GEORGE SANTAYANA

*ithout music, life would be a mistake...
I would only believe in a God that
knew how to dance.* FRIEDRICH NIETZSCHE

J am sessions, jitterbugs and cannibalistic rhythmic orgies are wooing our youth along the primrose path to Hell!

THE MOST REVEREND FRANCIS J.L. BECKMAN IN AN ADDRESS TO THE NATIONAL COUNCIL of CATHOLIC WOMEN, BILOXI, MISSISSIPPI, OCTOBER 25, 1938.

or I consider music a very innocent diversion, and perfectly compatible with the profession of a clergyman.

JANE AUSTEN

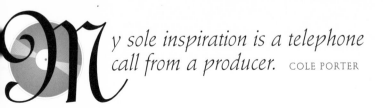

y sole inspiration is a telephone call from a producer. COLE PORTER

_____
_____
_____
_____
_____
_____
_____
_____
_____
_____
_____
_____
_____
_____
_____

Clara has written a number of smaller pieces which show a musicianship and a tenderness of invention such as she has never before attained. But children, and a husband who is always living in the realms of imagination, do not go well with composition. She cannot work at it regularly, and I am often disturbed to think how many tender ideas are lost because she cannot work them out.

ROBERT SCHUMANN

_____
_____
_____
_____
_____
_____
_____
_____
_____
_____
_____
_____
_____
_____
_____
_____
_____
_____
_____
_____
_____
_____
_____
_____

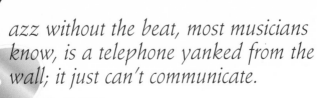

azz without the beat, most musicians know, is a telephone yanked from the wall; it just can't communicate.

LEONARD FEATHER

usic is no different from opium. Music affects the human mind in a way that makes people think of nothing but music and sensual matters. Opium produces one kind of sensitivity and lack of energy, music another kind...Music is a treason to our country, a treason to our youth, and we should cut out all this music and replace it with something constructive.

AYATOLLAH KHOMEINI

MUSIC
RECORD

TITLE

ARTIST

FORMAT / LABEL / YEAR

REVIEW / NOTES

RECOMMENDED BY / TO

TITLE

ARTIST

FORMAT / LABEL / YEAR

REVIEW / NOTES

RECOMMENDED BY / TO

TITLE

ARTIST

FORMAT / LABEL / YEAR

REVIEW / NOTES

RECOMMENDED BY / TO

TITLE

ARTIST

FORMAT / LABEL / YEAR

REVIEW / NOTES

RECOMMENDED BY / TO

TITLE

ARTIST

FORMAT / LABEL / YEAR

REVIEW / NOTES

RECOMMENDED BY / TO

 ould thou know if a people be well governed, if its laws be good or bad, examine the music it practices.

CONFUCIUS

TITLE

ARTIST

FORMAT / LABEL / YEAR

REVIEW / NOTES

RECOMMENDED BY / TO

TITLE

ARTIST

FORMAT / LABEL / YEAR

REVIEW / NOTES

RECOMMENDED BY / TO

TITLE

ARTIST

FORMAT / LABEL / YEAR

REVIEW / NOTES

RECOMMENDED BY / TO

MUSIC RECORD BY TITLE

TITLE

ARTIST

FORMAT / LABEL / YEAR

REVIEW / NOTES

RECOMMENDED BY / TO

TITLE

ARTIST

FORMAT / LABEL / YEAR

REVIEW / NOTES

RECOMMENDED BY / TO

usic is a means of unifying broad masses of people.

VLADIMIR ILYICH ULYANOV LENIN

TITLE

ARTIST

FORMAT / LABEL / YEAR

REVIEW / NOTES

RECOMMENDED BY / TO

TITLE

ARTIST

FORMAT / LABEL / YEAR

REVIEW / NOTES

RECOMMENDED BY / TO

*usic was invented to deceive
and delude mankind.*

EPHORUS, 4TH CENTURY BC

TITLE

ARTIST

FORMAT / LABEL / YEAR

REVIEW / NOTES

RECOMMENDED BY / TO

TITLE

ARTIST

FORMAT / LABEL / YEAR

REVIEW / NOTES

RECOMMENDED BY / TO

TITLE

ARTIST

FORMAT / LABEL / YEAR

REVIEW / NOTES

RECOMMENDED BY / TO

TITLE

ARTIST

FORMAT / LABEL / YEAR

REVIEW / NOTES

RECOMMENDED BY / TO

TITLE

ARTIST

FORMAT / LABEL / YEAR

REVIEW / NOTES

RECOMMENDED BY / TO

TITLE

ARTIST

FORMAT / LABEL / YEAR

REVIEW / NOTES

RECOMMENDED BY / TO

TITLE

ARTIST

FORMAT / LABEL / YEAR

REVIEW / NOTES

RECOMMENDED BY / TO

TITLE

ARTIST

FORMAT / LABEL / YEAR

REVIEW / NOTES

RECOMMENDED BY / TO

TITLE

ARTIST

FORMAT / LABEL / YEAR

REVIEW / NOTES

RECOMMENDED BY / TO

TITLE

ARTIST

FORMAT / LABEL / YEAR

REVIEW / NOTES

RECOMMENDED BY / TO

TITLE

ARTIST

FORMAT / LABEL / YEAR

REVIEW / NOTES

RECOMMENDED BY / TO

TITLE

ARTIST

FORMAT / LABEL / YEAR

REVIEW / NOTES

RECOMMENDED BY / TO

TITLE

ARTIST

FORMAT / LABEL / YEAR

REVIEW / NOTES

RECOMMENDED BY / TO

TITLE

ARTIST

FORMAT / LABEL / YEAR

REVIEW / NOTES

RECOMMENDED BY / TO

*usic was originally discreet,
seemly, simple, masculine, and
of good morals. Have not the
moderns rendered it lascivious beyond measure?*

JACOB OF LIEGE, 1425

TITLE

ARTIST

FORMAT / LABEL / YEAR

REVIEW / NOTES

RECOMMENDED BY / TO

TITLE

ARTIST

FORMAT / LABEL / YEAR

REVIEW / NOTES

RECOMMENDED BY / TO

TITLE

ARTIST

FORMAT / LABEL / YEAR

REVIEW / NOTES

RECOMMENDED BY / TO

TITLE

ARTIST

FORMAT / LABEL / YEAR

REVIEW / NOTES

RECOMMENDED BY / TO

TITLE

ARTIST

FORMAT / LABEL / YEAR

REVIEW / NOTES

RECOMMENDED BY / TO

 *usic is the occult metaphysical exercise of a soul not knowing that it philosophizes.*

ARTHUR SCHOPENHAUER

ARTIST	TITLE

ARTIST	TITLE

ARTIST	TITLE

ARTIST	TITLE

he indefatigable pursuit of an unattainable perfection, even though it consists in nothing more than in the pounding of an old piano, is what alone gives a meaning to our life on this unavailing star. LOGAN PEARSALL SMITH

ARTIST	TITLE

MUSIC RECORD BY ARTIST

ARTIST	TITLE

MUSIC RECORD BY ARTIST

ARTIST	TITLE

ARTIST	TITLE

omehow I suspect that if Shakespeare were alive today, he might be a jazz fan himself. DUKE ELLINGTON

ARTIST	TITLE

ARTIST	TITLE

y whole trick is to keep the tune well out in front. If I play Tchaikovsky I play his melodies and skip his spiritual struggles. Naturally I condense. I have to know just how many notes my audience will stand for. If there's time left over I fill in with a lot of runs up and down the keyboard. LIBERACE

MUSIC RECORD BY ARTIST

ARTIST	TITLE

STYLE:

TITLE   ARTIST

STYLE:

TITLE	ARTIST

STYLE:

TITLE   ARTIST

STYLE:

TITLE	ARTIST

n Chicago alone, the Illinois Vigilance association's representatives have traced the fall of 1,000 girls to jazz music.

NEW YORK AMERICAN, JANUARY 1922

STYLE:

TITLE   ARTIST

STYLE:

TITLE	ARTIST

STYLE:

TITLE	ARTIST

STYLE:

TITLE	ARTIST

The jazz mania has taken on the character of a lingering illness and must be cured by means of forceful public intervention.

BORIS GIBALIN, *IZVESTIA*, SEPT 28, 1958

It is the truth: comedians and jazz musicians have been more comforting and enlightening to me than preachers and politicians or philosophers or poets or painters or novelists of my time. Historians in the future, in my opinion, will congratulate us on very little other than our clowning and our jazz. KURT VONNEGUT, JR.

MUSICAL PERFORMANCES

DATE / VENUE / TIME

ARTIST

PROGRAM

REVIEW / NOTES

DATE / VENUE / TIME

ARTIST

PROGRAM

REVIEW / NOTES

DATE / VENUE / TIME

ARTIST

PROGRAM

REVIEW / NOTES

DATE / VENUE / TIME

ARTIST

PROGRAM

REVIEW / NOTES

DATE / VENUE / TIME

ARTIST

PROGRAM

REVIEW / NOTES

DATE / VENUE / TIME

ARTIST

PROGRAM

REVIEW / NOTES

DATE / VENUE / TIME

ARTIST

PROGRAM

REVIEW / NOTES

DATE / VENUE / TIME

ARTIST

PROGRAM

REVIEW / NOTES

DATE / VENUE / TIME

ARTIST

PROGRAM

REVIEW / NOTES

DATE / VENUE / TIME

ARTIST

PROGRAM

REVIEW / NOTES

DATE / VENUE / TIME

ARTIST

PROGRAM

REVIEW / NOTES

pera is where a guy gets stabbed in the back, and instead of dying, he sings.   ROBERT BENCHLEY

DATE / VENUE / TIME

ARTIST

PROGRAM

REVIEW / NOTES

DATE / VENUE / TIME

ARTIST

PROGRAM

REVIEW / NOTES

DATE / VENUE / TIME

ARTIST

PROGRAM

REVIEW / NOTES

DATE / VENUE / TIME

ARTIST

PROGRAM

REVIEW / NOTES

DATE / VENUE / TIME

ARTIST

PROGRAM

REVIEW / NOTES

DATE / VENUE / TIME

ARTIST

PROGRAM

REVIEW / NOTES

Ouf! Let me get out; I must have air. It's incredible! Marvellous! It has so upset and bewildered me that when I wanted to put on my hat, I couldn't find my head... One ought not to write music like that.

JEAN FRANCOIS LE SUEUR, 1865 [OF BEETHOVEN'S SYMPHONY NO. 5]

*usical training is a more potent
instrument than any other,
because rhythm and harmony
find their way into the secret places of the soul.*

PLATO

I conclude that musical notes and rhythms were first acquired by the male and female progenitors of mankind for the sake of charming the opposite sex. CHARLES DARWIN

MUSICAL
FRIENDS

MUSIC LOVER

GIFT IDEAS

OCCASION

MUSIC LOVER

GIFT IDEAS

OCCASION

MUSIC LOVER

GIFT IDEAS

OCCASION

MUSIC LOVER

GIFT IDEAS

OCCASION

MUSIC LOVER

GIFT IDEAS

OCCASION

MUSIC LOVER

GIFT IDEAS

OCCASION

MUSIC LOVER

GIFT IDEAS

OCCASION

MUSIC LOVER

GIFT IDEAS

OCCASION

MUSIC LOVER

GIFT IDEAS

OCCASION

ood music isn't nearly as bad as it sounds.

HARRY ZELZER

MUSIC LOVER

GIFT IDEAS

OCCASION

MUSIC LOVER

GIFT IDEAS

OCCASION

MUSIC LOVER

GIFT IDEAS

OCCASION

MUSIC LOVER

GIFT IDEAS

OCCASION

MUSIC LOVER

GIFT IDEAS

OCCASION

MUSIC LOVER

GIFT IDEAS

OCCASION

MUSIC LOVER

GIFT IDEAS

OCCASION

MUSIC LOVER

GIFT IDEAS

OCCASION

MUSIC LOVER

GIFT IDEAS

OCCASION

MUSIC LOVER

GIFT IDEAS

OCCASION

MUSIC LOVER

OCCASION

TITLE

ARTIST

MUSIC LOVER

OCCASION

TITLE

ARTIST

MUSIC LOVER

OCCASION

TITLE

ARTIST

MUSIC LOVER

OCCASION

TITLE

ARTIST

MUSIC LOVER

OCCASION

TITLE

ARTIST

MUSIC LOVER

OCCASION

TITLE

ARTIST

MUSIC LOVER

OCCASION

TITLE

ARTIST

MUSIC LOVER

OCCASION

TITLE

ARTIST

MUSIC LOVER

OCCASION

TITLE

ARTIST

MUSIC LOVER

OCCASION

TITLE

ARTIST

MUSIC LOVER

OCCASION

TITLE

ARTIST

MUSIC LOVER

OCCASION

TITLE

ARTIST

MUSIC LOVER

OCCASION

TITLE

ARTIST

MUSIC LOVER

OCCASION

TITLE

ARTIST

MUSIC LOVER

OCCASION

TITLE

ARTIST

MUSIC LOVER

OCCASION

TITLE

ARTIST

MUSIC LOVER

OCCASION

TITLE

ARTIST

MUSIC LOVER

OCCASION

TITLE

ARTIST

f any person has sung or composed against another person a song such as was causing slander or insult to another, he shall be clubbed to death.

ROMAN LAW, ROMAN TWELVE TABLES, 449 BC

TITLE

ARTIST

FROM

OCCASION

TITLE

ARTIST

FROM

OCCASION

TITLE

ARTIST

FROM

OCCASION

TITLE

ARTIST

FROM

OCCASION

TITLE

ARTIST

FROM

OCCASION

TITLE

ARTIST

FROM

OCCASION

TITLE

ARTIST

FROM

OCCASION

TITLE

ARTIST

FROM

OCCASION

TITLE

ARTIST

FROM

OCCASION

TITLE

ARTIST

FROM

OCCASION

MUSICAL FRIENDS   MUSIC RECEIVED AS GIFTS

TITLE

ARTIST

FROM

OCCASION

TITLE

ARTIST

FROM

OCCASION

TITLE

ARTIST

FROM

OCCASION

TITLE

ARTIST

FROM

OCCASION

TITLE

ARTIST

FROM

OCCASION

TITLE

ARTIST

FROM

OCCASION

TITLE

ARTIST

FROM

OCCASION

TITLE

ARTIST

FROM

OCCASION

TITLE

ARTIST

FROM

OCCASION

he most despairing songs are the most beautiful, and I know some immortal ones that are pure tears. ALFRED DE MUSSET

TITLE

ARTIST

LENDER

DATE BORROWED   DATE RETURNED

TITLE

ARTIST

LENDER

DATE BORROWED   DATE RETURNED

TITLE

ARTIST

LENDER

DATE BORROWED   DATE RETURNED

TITLE

ARTIST

LENDER

DATE BORROWED   DATE RETURNED

TITLE

ARTIST

LENDER

DATE BORROWED   DATE RETURNED

TITLE

ARTIST

LENDER

DATE BORROWED   DATE RETURNED

TITLE

ARTIST

LENDER

DATE BORROWED   DATE RETURNED

TITLE

ARTIST

LENDER

DATE BORROWED   DATE RETURNED

TITLE

ARTIST

LENDER

DATE BORROWED   DATE RETURNED

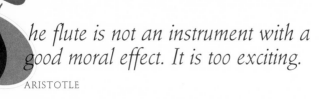

he flute is not an instrument with a good moral effect. It is too exciting.

ARISTOTLE

TITLE

ARTIST

LENDER

DATE BORROWED   DATE RETURNED

TITLE

ARTIST

LENDER

DATE BORROWED   DATE RETURNED

TITLE

ARTIST

LENDER

DATE BORROWED   DATE RETURNED

TITLE

ARTIST

LENDER

DATE BORROWED   DATE RETURNED

TITLE

ARTIST

LENDER

DATE BORROWED   DATE RETURNED

TITLE

ARTIST

LENDER

DATE BORROWED   DATE RETURNED

TITLE

ARTIST

LENDER

DATE BORROWED   DATE RETURNED

TITLE

ARTIST

LENDER

DATE BORROWED   DATE RETURNED

TITLE

ARTIST

LENDER

DATE BORROWED   DATE RETURNED

TITLE

ARTIST

LENDER

DATE BORROWED   DATE RETURNED

TITLE

ARTIST

BORROWER

DATE BORROWED   DATE RETURNED

TITLE

ARTIST

BORROWER

DATE BORROWED   DATE RETURNED

TITLE

ARTIST

BORROWER

DATE BORROWED   DATE RETURNED

TITLE

ARTIST

BORROWER

DATE BORROWED   DATE RETURNED

*ho hears music, feels his solitude
Peopled at once.*

ROBERT BROWNING

TITLE

ARTIST

BORROWER

DATE BORROWED   DATE RETURNED

TITLE

ARTIST

BORROWER

DATE BORROWED   DATE RETURNED

TITLE

ARTIST

BORROWER

DATE BORROWED   DATE RETURNED

TITLE

ARTIST

BORROWER

DATE BORROWED   DATE RETURNED

TITLE

ARTIST

BORROWER

DATE BORROWED   DATE RETURNED

TITLE

ARTIST

BORROWER

DATE BORROWED   DATE RETURNED

TITLE

ARTIST

BORROWER

DATE BORROWED   DATE RETURNED

TITLE

ARTIST

BORROWER

DATE BORROWED   DATE RETURNED

TITLE

ARTIST

BORROWER

DATE BORROWED   DATE RETURNED

TITLE

ARTIST

BORROWER

DATE BORROWED   DATE RETURNED

TITLE

ARTIST

BORROWER

DATE BORROWED   DATE RETURNED

TITLE

ARTIST

BORROWER

DATE BORROWED   DATE RETURNED

TITLE

ARTIST

BORROWER

DATE BORROWED   DATE RETURNED

TITLE

ARTIST

BORROWER

DATE BORROWED   DATE RETURNED

*hen I hear music, I fear no danger.
I am invulnerable. I see no foe.
I am related to the earliest times,
and to the latest.* H.D. THOREAU

When I think of anything properly describable as a beautiful idea, it is always in the form of music. I have written and printed probably 10,000,000 words in English...but all the same I shall die an inarticulate man, for my best ideas beset me in a language I know only vaguely and speak only as a child.

H.L. MENCKEN

MUSICAL
ACCOMPANI-
MENT

TITLE

ARTIST

PUBLISHER / PUB. DATE

NOTES

TITLE

ARTIST

PUBLISHER / PUB. DATE

NOTES

TITLE

ARTIST

PUBLISHER / PUB. DATE

NOTES

TITLE

ARTIST

PUBLISHER / PUB. DATE

NOTES

TITLE

ARTIST

PUBLISHER / PUB. DATE

NOTES

TITLE

ARTIST

PUBLISHER / PUB. DATE

NOTES

TITLE

ARTIST

PUBLISHER / PUB. DATE

NOTES

TITLE

ARTIST

PUBLISHER / PUB. DATE

NOTES

TITLE

ARTIST

PUBLISHER / PUB. DATE

NOTES

TITLE

ARTIST

PUBLISHER / PUB. DATE

NOTES

TITLE

ARTIST

PUBLISHER / PUB. DATE

NOTES

TITLE

ARTIST

PUBLISHER / PUB. DATE

NOTES

TITLE

ARTIST

PUBLISHER / PUB. DATE

NOTES

TITLE

ARTIST

PUBLISHER / PUB. DATE

NOTES

TITLE

ARTIST

PUBLISHER / PUB. DATE

NOTES

TITLE

ARTIST

PUBLISHER / PUB. DATE

NOTES

TITLE

ARTIST

PUBLISHER / PUB. DATE

NOTES

TITLE

ARTIST

PUBLISHER / PUB. DATE

NOTES

I t is quite possible to lead a virtuous and happy life without books, or ink; but not without wishing to sing, when we are happy; not without meeting with continual occasions when our song, if right, would be a kind service to others. JOHN RUSKIN

AUTHOR	TITLE

AUTHOR	TITLE

AUTHOR	TITLE

AUTHOR	TITLE

 *would much rather have written the best song of a nation than its noblest epic.* EDGAR ALLAN POE

SUBJECT:

TITLE   AUTHOR

I want to say something comforting in the way that music is comforting... In the end we shall have had enough of cynicism and scepticism and humbug and we shall want to live more musically.

VINCENT VAN GOGH

SUBJECT:

TITLE   AUTHOR

SUBJECT:

TITLE	AUTHOR

SUBJECT:

TITLE   AUTHOR

TITLE

SUBJECT

NOTES

TITLE

SUBJECT

NOTES

TITLE

SUBJECT

NOTES

TITLE

SUBJECT

NOTES

TITLE

SUBJECT

NOTES

TITLE

SUBJECT

NOTES

TITLE

SUBJECT

NOTES

TITLE

SUBJECT

NOTES

TITLE

SUBJECT

NOTES

 *ritics can't even make music by rubbing their back legs together.*

MEL BROOKS

SUBJECT:

TITLE

SUBJECT:

TITLE

_have found through my experiences
that critics know what you're thinking
or trying to portray as much as a baby
in Afghanistan would understand when you
speak English._ DIZZY GILLESPIE

TITLE

ADDRESS / PHONE

SUBSCRIPTION #

SUBSCRIPTION BEGINS / ENDS

TITLE

ADDRESS / PHONE

SUBSCRIPTION #

SUBSCRIPTION BEGINS / ENDS

TITLE

ADDRESS / PHONE

SUBSCRIPTION #

SUBSCRIPTION BEGINS / ENDS

TITLE

ADDRESS / PHONE

SUBSCRIPTION #

SUBSCRIPTION BEGINS / ENDS

TITLE

ADDRESS / PHONE

SUBSCRIPTION #

SUBSCRIPTION BEGINS / ENDS

TITLE

ADDRESS / PHONE

SUBSCRIPTION #

SUBSCRIPTION BEGINS / ENDS

TITLE

ADDRESS / PHONE

SUBSCRIPTION #

SUBSCRIPTION BEGINS / ENDS

TITLE

ADDRESS / PHONE

SUBSCRIPTION #

SUBSCRIPTION BEGINS / ENDS

TITLE

ADDRESS / PHONE

SUBSCRIPTION #

SUBSCRIPTION BEGINS / ENDS

TITLE

ADDRESS / PHONE

SUBSCRIPTION #

SUBSCRIPTION BEGINS / ENDS

Music is the short-hand of emotion. Emotions which let themselves be described in words with such difficulty, are directly conveyed to man in music, and in that is its power and significance.

LEO TOLSTOY

MUSIC
LISTS

Nothing pleases the composer so much as to have people disagree as to the movements of his piece that they liked best. If there is enough disagreement, it means that everyone liked something best – which is just what the composer wants to hear. The fact that this might include parts that no one liked never seems to matter.

AARON COPLAND

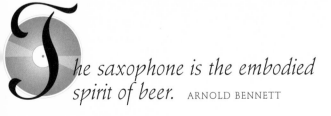

he saxophone is the embodied spirit of beer. ARNOLD BENNETT

_M_ usic, in the best sense, does not require novelty; nay, the older it is, and the more we are accustomed to it, the greater its effect. JOHANN WOLFGANG VON GOETHE

Songs are sneaky things. They can slip across borders. Proliferate in prisons. Penetrate hard shells...I always believed that the right song at the right moment could change history. PETE SEEGER

LYRICAL
PASSAGES

LYRICAL PASSAGES

If music be the food
of love, play on;
Give me excess of it, that,
surfeiting,
The appetite may sicken,
and so die.
That strain again!
It had a dying fall:
O! it came o'er my ear
like the sweet sound
That breathes upon
a bank of violets,
Stealing and giving odour!

WILLIAM SHAKESPEARE, *TWELFTH NIGHT*

MUSICAL
PLACES

NAME

ADDRESS

PHONE

NOTES

NAME

ADDRESS

PHONE

NOTES

NAME

ADDRESS

PHONE

NOTES

NAME

ADDRESS

PHONE

NOTES

NAME

ADDRESS

PHONE

NOTES

NAME

ADDRESS

PHONE

NOTES

NAME

ADDRESS

PHONE

NOTES

NAME

ADDRESS

PHONE

NOTES

NAME

ADDRESS

PHONE

NOTES

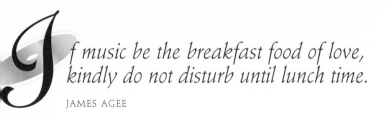

f music be the breakfast food of love,
kindly do not disturb until lunch time.

JAMES AGEE

NAME

ADDRESS

PHONE

NOTES

NAME

ADDRESS

PHONE

NOTES

NAME

ADDRESS

PHONE

NOTES

NAME

ADDRESS

PHONE

NOTES

NAME

ADDRESS

PHONE

NOTES

NAME

ADDRESS

PHONE

NOTES

NAME

ADDRESS

PHONE

NOTES

NAME

ADDRESS

PHONE

NOTES

NAME

ADDRESS

PHONE

NOTES

NAME

ADDRESS

PHONE

NOTES

NAME

VENUE / DATES

PHONE

NOTES

NAME

VENUE / DATES

PHONE

NOTES

NAME

VENUE / DATES

PHONE

NOTES

NAME

VENUE / DATES

PHONE

NOTES

NAME

VENUE / DATES

PHONE

NOTES

NAME

VENUE / DATES

PHONE

NOTES

NAME

VENUE / DATES

PHONE

NOTES

NAME

VENUE / DATES

PHONE

NOTES

NAME

VENUE / DATES

PHONE

NOTES

NAME

VENUE / DATES

PHONE

NOTES

SHOW

STATION / FREQUENCY

TIME

NOTES

SHOW

STATION / FREQUENCY

TIME

NOTES

SHOW

STATION / FREQUENCY

TIME

NOTES

SHOW

STATION / FREQUENCY

TIME

NOTES

love Beethoven, especially the poems.

RINGO STARR